ANCIENT ADVENTURES

WALES

Edited By Machaela Gavaghan

First published in Great Britain in 2019 by:

Young Writers
Remus House
Coltsfoot Drive
Peterborough
PE2 9BF
Telephone: 01733 890066
Website: www.youngwriters.co.uk

All Rights Reserved
Book Design by Ashley Janson
© Copyright Contributors 2019
Softback ISBN 978-1-83928-049-8
Hardback ISBN 978-1-83928-050-4
Printed and bound in the UK by BookPrintingUK
Website: www.bookprintinguk.com
YB0420B

FOREWORD

Welcome, Reader!

Are you ready to step back in time? Then come right this way - your time-travelling machine awaits! It's very simple, all you have to do is turn the page and you'll be transported to the past! WOW!

Is it magic? Is it a trick? No! It's all down to the skill and imagination of primary school pupils from around the country. We gave them the task of writing a story about any time in history, and to do it in just 100 words! I think you'll agree they've achieved that brilliantly – this book is jam-packed with exciting and thrilling tales from the past.

These young authors have brought history to life with their stories. This is the power of creativity and it gives us life too! Here at Young Writers we want to pass our love of the written word onto the next generation and what better way to do that than to celebrate their writing by publishing it in a book!

It sets their work free from homework books and notepads and puts it where it deserves to be – out in the world and preserved forever! Each awesome author in this book should be super proud of themselves, and now they've got proof of their imagination, their ideas and their creativity in black and white, to look back on in years to come when their first experience of publication is an ancient adventure itself!

Now I'm off to dive through the timelines and pick some winners – it's going to be difficult to choose, but I'm going to have a lot of fun along the way. I may even learn some new history facts too!

Machaela

CONTENTS

Gors Community School, Cockett

Lamar Abdullah Alkemis (8)	1
Ryan Parry James (9)	2
Damien Ayres (9)	3
Ellie Lobb-McQueen (10)	4
Tia-Rose Minns (10)	5
Maddison Kate Davies (10)	6
Tanisha Lerwell (10)	7
Keira Thomas (10)	8
Bailey Jay Parry (10)	9
Oscar Chen (10)	10
Caden Beck (9)	11
Austin Mastalerz (10)	12
Jenna Gear (9)	13
Tegan Beynon (8)	14
Mason Goldsworthy (9)	15
Danny Piya Gwynne (10)	16
Skye Davies-Hinder (9)	17

Holton Primary School, Barry

Brooke Elise Cahill (9)	18
Peter Salter (9)	19
Rhiannon Louise Edwards (9)	20
Ruby Taylor (9)	21
Jaiden Herrington (9)	22
Nathan Tudor (9)	23
Thansin Aung (9)	24
Ryan Woodfield (9)	25
Sion Davies-Woodfield (9)	26
Tanisha Ahmed (9)	27
Ellie-Marie Roberts (9)	28

Cleopatra Alice Perry (9)	29
Nadia Hasan (9)	30
Harris Childs-Brown (9)	31
Harry James David Waters (9)	32
Ethan Christopher Barnett (9)	33
Michael Kong (8)	34
Harry Herbert (9)	35

Pontprennau Primary School, Pontprennau

Kavya Kedia (7)	36
Jack Parker (7)	37
Aryav Khurana (8)	38
Lilly-Mai Ford (8)	39
Jahnavi Batra (8)	40
Beth Parker (8)	41
Charlie Lewys Cummings (8)	42

Redhill Preparatory School, Haverfordwest

Gabriel Gale (8)	43
Annabel John (9)	44
Megan Bateman (9)	45
Katie John (9)	46
Pirasanna Akshayan (8)	47
Ioan Connor Ireland (10)	48
Isabella Crystal Lily Harries (10)	49
Bethan Lusher (10)	50
Seren Kaill (9)	51
Sangavi Rajaseelan (9)	52
Kathryn Elin Thomas (9)	53
Isabella Frost (8)	54

Lily Lawrence (11)	55
Isabella Vickers (9)	56
Harry Thomas (8)	57
Sam Hutton (9)	58
Ali Gouda (10)	59
Finlay McQueen (9)	60
Deema Al-Samra (10)	61
Erin Frost (10)	62
Freddie Watson-Miller (10)	63
Harri Coaker (9)	64
Max Ironside (10)	65
Emma Edwards (8)	66
Charles Muehlbauer (9)	67
Darcy Louise Flynn (8)	68
Seth Appleby (8)	69
Charlie Hughes (10)	70

St David's RC Primary School, West Cross

Ruairi Harris (10)	71
Lucy Maslen (10)	72
Rhun Hywel Mugford (10)	73
Mia Denti Richards (10)	74
Eloghosa Ikpomwosa-Aghedo (10)	75
Isabella Cushion (10)	76
Sofia Elena Ramos (10)	77
Daniel Hughes (10)	78
Joshua Ellis Evans (10)	79
Ellis James Williams (10)	80
Luca Jenson Armani (10)	81
Tom Joseph Hedden (10)	82
Eve Evans (10)	83
Patrick Rawls (10)	84
Eva Rowlands (10)	85
Oisin Tobin (10)	86
Hannah Kielthy (10)	87
Samit Sajeev (10)	88
Matilda Elizabeth Lewis (10)	89
Charlie Edwards	90

Treffos Independent School, Llansadwrn

Madison Bermingham (11)	91

Trelales Primary School, Laleston

Freya Hughes (9)	92
Chloe Thomas-Lane (9)	93
Hermione Farmer (9)	94
Sean Finnie (8)	95
Benjamin Jones (9)	96
Niamh Hemburrow (9)	97
Mason Brown (9)	98
Rosie Harry (9)	99
Delyth Foster (9)	100
Ioan Hughes Davies (9)	101
Thomas Edward Morgan (9)	102
Jake Hamilton (9)	103
Gracie Kearns (9)	104
Gethin Lewis Narbeth (9)	105
Callum Joseph Threfall (9)	106
Coby Jervis (9)	107
Jake Ellams (9)	108
William Waite (9)	109

Ysgol Bro Ingli, Newport

Izzy Ellie Bartram (10)	110
Alex English (10)	111
Hari Nambisan (11)	112
Nathaniel Elmes (11)	113

Ysgol Gynradd Mynach, Devils Bridge

Peni Macy (9)	114
Tomos Hopkins (8)	115
Elain Jenkins (11)	116
Alfie Fredrick Herbert (9)	117
Laila Hale (9)	118

Evie Hale (9) 119

Ysgol Parcyrhun, Ammanford

Harriet Tozer (8) 120
Rhiane Turton (11) 121
Steffan Rhys Thomas (8) 122

Ysgol Ty Ffynnon, Shotton

Kuba Andrzej Mrugala (10) 123
Emmelia Rose Paterson (10) 124
Archie Duncan (10) 125
Jack Kearns (10) 126
Tatiana Gorecka (10) 127
Isabelle Alâna Jones (10) 128
Mariusz Boldowski (10) 129
Teigan O'Driscoll (10) 130
Daniel McHarg (10) 131
Hayden Davies (10) 132
Victoria Cecot (10) 133
Aidyn Edward Potter (10) 134
Natalia Sokolowska (10) 135
Ella Jane (10) 136

THE MINI SAGAS

Mummies

"Look there!" shouted Rick. "There are some dead people!"

"Let's take them to the pyramids and turn them into mummies," replied Simon.

Firstly, they needed to wet them in the River Nile. *Splash, splash!* Finished. Secondly, they needed to take them to the pyramids and put salt or spice on the bodies. *Sprinkle, sprinkle!* Finished. Next, they needed to get a hook and put it through the people's noses. *Rrr! Rrr!* Finished.

After that, they needed to cut some of the people's bodies. *Rip, rip!* Finished. Next, they needed to mummify the bodies. *Mummify, mummify!* Finished. "Wow, we're finished!"

Lamar Abdullah Alkemis (8)
Gors Community School, Cockett

The Night Of The Living Mummy

There was a new mummy - Xerxes, the last Pharaoh. Tutankhamun became Pharaoh. Now Xerxes hated Tutankhamun. After being killed by an assassin, he thought that Tutankhamun had murdered him just so he could become king of Egypt. Xerxes was a god so he could come back to life as a mummy.

Later that night, Tutankhamun and his wife, Nefertiti, enjoyed being the new rulers of Egypt. A townsman was looking outside.

"Argh!"

A mummy was walking about, heading for Tutankhamun's house. *Bam!* He broke the door and snatched Nefertiti...

Ryan Parry James (9)
Gors Community School, Cockett

The Jurassic Explorer

Back in the Jurassic period, there lived a boy called Jeff and he loved exploring... until a dinosaur called Toothless chased him through the woods! He quickly ran behind a big tree. Jeff turned to check if he was there. *Bam!* They both bumped into each other.

Jeff woke up like a drunk worm coming out of the mud. Toothless stayed by Jeff the whole time he was knocked out. Jeff went to get some food but he didn't know Toothless was following him. Once he found Toothless was following him, he trained him to be his best friend forever.

Damien Ayres (9)
Gors Community School, Cockett

World War Two

The leader of Germany (Hitler) was walking the streets, waiting for somebody strong to fight him. He found two robust teenagers that also wanted a fight, so all three of them made their way up to the highest building. Suddenly, Jacob threw a dreadful punch and it hit Hitler in the stomach. As soon as Tommy turned around, Hitler kicked him aggressively in the leg. *Punch! Kick! Slap!* Hitler got injured easily. Hitler quickly got up and punched, kicked and slapped Jacob and Tommy. Tommy and Jacob booted Hitler; he went flying over the edge.

Ellie Lobb-McQueen (10)
Gors Community School, Cockett

Victoria's End

Queen Victoria's day was a dreadful and disastrous day. She gave up the throne. First, she woke up and she had an interesting idea in her head. She thought, *do I really want to be a queen?* Prince Albert came in and she explained how she was feeling about her decision.

The next day, Queen Victoria announced that she was giving up the throne. Her servant came up with an idea; the servant wanted to be queen, but she knew that Prince Albert would be next in line. The mystical servant would make sure she was next, no matter what...

Tia-Rose Minns (10)
Gors Community School, Cockett

Fred And Dingo

Fred was hungry. A little white rabbit caught the corner of his eye. He slowly moved closer to the animal but couldn't help himself. He tried to jump on the rabbit but the rabbit saw it coming and ran away. Fred was chasing the animal, the furry creature stopped. Fred tripped over the rabbit and bumped into a ferocious dinosaur, asleep, but he'd woken him up. The dinosaur chased Fred. He ran so fast, but all the dinosaur wanted to do was help him catch the food!
The dinosaur stopped him and said, "Hi, I'm Dingo!"

Maddison Kate Davies (10)
Gors Community School, Cockett

Victorians

Today was a mixed day. I woke up with people at the door saying about a party for the Victorians.
I, Queen Victoria, said, "What type of party is it?"
"A food and drinks party," they said.
"Okay then, I am going to wear my white, lovely dress today."
I bumped into Prince Albert at the party when I was eating my food. Everyone was enjoying themselves, talking, eating and even laughing! Prince Albert had to go. He came up to me and said the food was disgusting and he hated the party!

Tanisha Lerwell (10)
Gors Community School, Cockett

The Underworld

I stood in the leafy meadow, scythe gripped, looking for crops to harvest and animals to kill. In the long grass, I saw a golden fleece and I killed it swiftly. Suddenly, I blacked out.

I woke up in a dying meadow. I frantically ran around, trying to find a way out of the never-ending meadow, looking everywhere.

After a while, I finally found an exit and ran. I didn't look back. All I could think about was escaping. But I skidded to a halt as I reached a blood-red river because I saw a figure; it was Hades...

Keira Thomas (10)
Gors Community School, Cockett

Mystic Treasure

The sand blew, rocks moved as I raced for cover under the pyramid. As I got in, I saw the most beautiful and glorious treasure in my entire life. I started to grab some treasure. I picked up coins, trophies, gold blocks, shiny gems and some amazing diamonds. Then, as I turned my head, I saw creepy red eyes. I ran with fear with all my treasure. I dropped some treasure. I dropped some coins, shiny gems and gold blocks, but I survived with some treasure.

Finally, I saw some daylight through a small door...

Bailey Jay Parry (10)
Gors Community School, Cockett

Hungry Cavemen

Today was a great and lucky day. It started with two courageous cavemen going to hunt for food. Suddenly, they saw a great, big lion, it was eating a helpless bird and was roaring with power for attention. They wanted to catch it quickly and cook it, so they started digging a hole and covering the top with leaves. Then they got its attention and made it run over the hole. The moment came when the lion was trapped in the hole and they killed it. After that day, they were confident to trap any animal.

Oscar Chen (10)
Gors Community School, Cockett

The T-Rex And The Stegosaurus

In a forest on an island called Jurassic, T-rex and Stegosaurus were napping under a tree. When the sun came up, they woke up. They headed out into the forest to look for food to make them strong. They had to look at every tree to find berries. They found lots of them! T-rex and Stegosaurus pushed the tree to the ground to get the berries.
When the two dinosaurs had eaten their berries, they were full. They went back to their tree and back to sleep when the sun went down.

Caden Beck (9)
Gors Community School, Cockett

The Mummies

It was a pleasing day at the river that ran through Egypt. I saw something strange in the sand. Suddenly, mummies began to come out of the sand! I shouted and ran.

I finally got away and after thirty minutes, the mummies went back to go into the ground and I was safe. I went to my small Egyptian house and slept.

The next day, I was surprised because mummies were everywhere! I tried to escape. I ran as fast as I could. I ran and ran until I got away.

Austin Mastalerz (10)
Gors Community School, Cockett

The Mummy Who Came To Life

"Argh!"

The gritty sand was roasting. I could see the sandy steps that led to a point. The mummifier was mummifying a dead body, children were playing on the pyramids. All of a sudden, we heard a thunderous bang. It was a... mummy! The mad king called the Romans. The mummy destroyed one of the stepped pyramids. The mad king said to kill the mummy and they dramatically did.

"Thank god he is dead!" said the king.

Jenna Gear (9)
Gors Community School, Cockett

Nefertiti

It was a hot, dusty day when myself and Tutankhamun went to the temple to talk to Xerxes I about Greece, trading animals and food, but then his child walked up to us... Oh no, he'd turned Tutankhamun's wife, Nefertiti, into a mummy! "You've turned my royal wife into a mummy!" They wrapped her and then put her into a tomb specially decorated for her. Tutankhamun was super lucky because he had another wife!

Tegan Beynon (8)
Gors Community School, Cockett

The Heartless Mummy

We were in this amazing time with sand glistening all over. We were weighing the heart of Tutankhamun. The heart faded away, his eyes twinkled, he absorbed the powers of the gods, then the gods ran away.
At the ceremony of Prince Moses becoming pharaoh, the gods soon explained what happened. Prince Moses read a spell to summon a vortex. The mummy smashed it and tried to run away, but it was sucked up and never seen again...

Mason Goldsworthy (9)
Gors Community School, Cockett

WWI

It was a risky day. I was working with my friend, Noah, then I heard an explosion. I went downstairs and hid under the desk.
Then one of the soldiers came and said, "Come, we need you."
He took me and Noah to dress like one of the soldiers and gave me a gun.
After that, we started the war.
After three years, the USA joined the fight with France and the world. We fought from 1914-1918.

Danny Piya Gwynne (10)
Gors Community School, Cockett

Mummies In The Afterlife

I was in Egypt when I saw a tent full of bandages. I was a popular Egyptian queen. I was beautiful and super-rich because I was the pharaoh's wife. I was the only Cleopatra.

The last thing I could remember was my husband stabbing me with a big, sharp knife. I was found dead in the palace's throne room. I was quickly mummified and no evidence was found!

Skye Davies-Hinder (9)
Gors Community School, Cockett

Egypt

Hmm, what's that sound? Emperor Claudius and Cleopatra thought. Emperor Claudius stared at Cleopatra's short black hair and her brown gazing eyes. She walked away and suddenly disappeared into an angry mob of mummies!

"No!" screamed Emperor Claudius.

Then he saw a giant boulder coming after the angry mob.

"Cleo!" cried Emperor Claudius.

Emperor Claudius ran after the boulder. He caught up with the boulder. Some of the mob saw him. They started to beat him up.

After the fight, everything was gone.

He started to cry, "Cleo!"

He cried and screamed at Cleo's funeral.

Brooke Elise Cahill (9)
Holton Primary School, Barry

The Kraken

On a cold, dark night, I was in the engine room. It was warm in there, then *thump!* Something hit the boat. I tried to work the engine but it snapped. I ran to Joe.

I said, "Joe, the engine is broken."

We went outside, then we saw this huge octopus.

"It's the Kraken!" said Peter.

"Hurry, get an escape boat!"

"No, it's broken!" said Peter. "Get on the other escape boat!"

I tripped over. I grabbed Joe's hand.

"No one is left behind," said Joe.

"Thank you!" I said.

Peter Salter (9)
Holton Primary School, Barry

Blue

Me and my twin brother, Sam, were excited because we were going to Jurassic Park to see the brachiosaurus. His name was Blue.

As soon as we got through the gates, a shiver went down my spine. *Roar!* A dinosaur was moaning in pain. We all followed the sound.

"Oh no," I said, "that's a big cut!"

"I'll get the dino-aid!" shouted the dino guide.

He came back very fast and he stitched Blue up.

"Sorry kids, you'll have to come back another day. It'll be free next time."

Everybody said bye.

Rhiannon Louise Edwards (9)
Holton Primary School, Barry

King Arthur And The Unicorn

King Arthur was in his garden and found a unicorn that could talk.

The unicorn said, "Hello, Arthur. I heard you want to pull the Excalibur out of the stone."

"How would you know that?"

"It doesn't matter. Anyway, how do I do it?" said Arthur.

The unicorn said, "Faith."

Then it left. With this information, King Arthur went to his castle to the stone and pulled the sword out from it. From then on, he never doubted himself and always remembered to have faith in himself no matter what because of the unicorn.

Ruby Taylor (9)
Holton Primary School, Barry

Land Of The Dinosaurs

Me and Jimmy were stuck in time with dinosaurs. We ran into the deep, dark woods and climbed a colossal tree. We were accompanied by an apatosaurus. Then we fell into a deep sleep.
After sleeping, we climbed down and followed the apatosaurus.
Later, a suchomimus came and scared the apatosaurus and aimed its threatening eyes at us. We ran to the other side of the terrible forest. Out of nowhere, a carnotaurus ran over and tackled the suchominus. While they were fighting to the death, the carnotaurus was victorious and we found the time machine. We went home fast.

Jaiden Herrington (9)
Holton Primary School, Barry

The Colosseum

As John entered the immense Colosseum, he was ready to fight three fierce wolves! He was very determined to win and he miraculously defeated the three wolves! Julius Caesar was extremely impressed.

After that, they brought out the tough, mighty, undefeated five water buffalo! The big water buffalo were always successful. No one had beaten them, but John charged angrily with his sharp, pointed trident and the water buffalo charged with a giant clash of smoke and dust. When it cleared, they all saw John was successful. Julius Caesar thought it was outstanding.

Nathan Tudor (9)
Holton Primary School, Barry

Titanoboa Attack!

Long ago lived a swirly, scaly Titanoboa. Max and Lisa wanted to explore the rainforest.
"No big deal!" said Max, so off they went to the rainforest.
The Titanoboa stayed there silently. Max wanted to go to the dangerous path but Lisa wanted to go with the beautiful nature. They both split up. The path Max went on was the path where the Titanoboa was sleeping. Max tiptoed away but the Titanoboa woke up and bit Max. Lisa heard Max scream and made a trap. Lisa walked to Max and lifted him up. The Titanoboa slithered into the trap.

Thansin Aung (9)
Holton Primary School, Barry

The Story About Tyrannosaurus

In London, there was a museum. In it, there was a terrifying tyrannosaurus. Nobody knew but it was alive. Every night, the tyrannosaurus tried to get out but on April 30th 1119, the tyrannosaurus got out and broke a lot of the valuable stuff.

The next day, the museum called the police to investigate. The police saw that a lot of stuff had been destroyed. The police were shocked. It was trying to be a statue.

In the night, the tyrannosaurus went to the sand and then the diplodocus showed up. That's when something really bad happened...

Ryan Woodfield (9)
Holton Primary School, Barry

Ice

There are two creatures and a human. They are trying to survive the Ice Age. The ice cracks and the penguins are squealing. The ice is cracking on the steep, freezing hill. The ice is broken.
"Argh!" says Sion. "I'm falling into the ocean!"
"No!" says the creature.
Splash! They are in the depths of the southern ocean. They are swimming up and up. Then a bird comes flying down, the fastest bird. It flies them over the globe to Africa! They get to Libya and they are happy!

Sion Davies-Woodfield (9)
Holton Primary School, Barry

The Dinosaur And The Caveman

In a deep, dark jungle, there lived a caveman and a dinosaur. The caveman did not like the dinosaur so he moved to a cave. But once, he saw the dinosaur. He ran as fast as he could, he ran like lightning! *What should I do?* But the dinosaur felt sad.
"Did I do something?" said the caveman.
The caveman had a thought. He didn't have any friends. He thought he could be friends with the dinosaur, so he looked in the jungle to find him. He found him. The dinosaur was happy. They were friends.

Tanisha Ahmed (9)
Holton Primary School, Barry

The Colosseum

One day, I was working in the Colosseum. The slaves were following me. I asked what was wrong. They said the animals were gone. I didn't understand. The slaves said it again.
"All the animals have gone missing!"
I tried to find them but sadly, they were gone. I walked and walked. I looked for hours and hours. I went upstairs. The animals weren't there. I walked outside. What did I see? I saw the beautiful, strong animals! I was so surprised. My slaves took them back to their cages.

Ellie-Marie Roberts (9)
Holton Primary School, Barry

The Queen

One day, one typical day, Queen Elizabeth I decided to go to church, not unusual. So she got ready and got in her carriage.

When she was going to church, she got stuck in a carriage jam. But when everyone was shifting along, she couldn't move! She glared down and saw that she would fall into horse droppings! She couldn't get out! She was stuck there, in the smelly horse droppings! She did not know how to get out, so the carriage driver had to try and lift her out, but he couldn't lift her!

Cleopatra Alice Perry (9)
Holton Primary School, Barry

The Mysterious Adventure At The Colosseum

One day, I was working in the Colosseum, then I was about to get the animals to fight but they weren't there! I called my slaves to search where they could've gone.

Meanwhile, I had to close the Colosseum. I went down to see if they'd found anything. A slave came to me and said that there was a hole. Another slave went outside and there were the animals. He slammed the doors open and told us. We all ran out and started catching them, it was hectic. Thankfully, we could open the Colosseum.

Nadia Hasan (9)
Holton Primary School, Barry

The Gladiator Chase

There were two boys called Harris and Harry. It was a foggy day and they were walking to the Colosseum. But then gladiators were chasing them! It was a dead end but they found a path to the jungle. They climbed vines, the gladiators did the same. Harry and Harris tripped up and the gladiators pointed their swords at them. But then they found swords and fought them. It was a hard fight but Harris and Harry won the fight. But then a monster came from the ground. They needed to destroy it...

Harris Childs-Brown (9)
Holton Primary School, Barry

The Titanoboa

Once, ten million years ago, there lived a Titanoboa. Lucy and Max had always tried to capture the Titanoboa. They weren't the only ones trying to capture the Titanoboa until one day, Lucy and Max were asleep. The Titanoboa started taking their food and water. The village was sad, so Lucy and Max had to think of an idea...

After a couple of days, Max thought of an idea. The idea was to put meat on the floor. Max and Lucy hung on a tree and the Titanoboa got trapped, then killed.

Harry James David Waters (9)
Holton Primary School, Barry

The Roman Gladiators

One morning, I went to fight as a gladiator. As I was fighting, a beast came into the Colosseum. Oh no, the beast ate people! The gladiators got an army to fight the beast. The beast looked like Godzilla. Our army was fierce and petrifying. The gladiators tried to stab the beast but the beast just attacked us. Many were injured or dead. We tried again but he attacked. We went back to get our army, then we stabbed him in the heart and he died.
Everyone shouted, "Hooray!"

Ethan Christopher Barnett (9)
Holton Primary School, Barry

The Fire Dragon

I trudged into a deep, dark, damp, gloomy forest and I saw an ancient beast. It had flaming, beady, fierce eyes, sharp, pointy scales, knife claws, shiny, nailed teeth and it was enormous. It bolted to me and I ran fast. The dragon thundered furiously. It spat out hot, steaming, flaming fire and it zoomed like a fire golden star. Then I sprinted like a cannonball. It almost got me, then I found a safe place. The terrifying, creepy, lava flame dragon flew away.

Michael Kong (8)
Holton Primary School, Barry

The Gladiators

There were two twelve-year-olds, their names were Harry and Harris. Harry was the hard one, Harris was the brave one. They were the best of friends. One day, they wanted to become gladiators, so they became them.

Four years later, they were so popular. They were allowed to be called 'the best'.

One day, they started to get booed so they ran away from Rome to the USA and stayed in the jungle. It was so cold, they kept running...

Harry Herbert (9)
Holton Primary School, Barry

The Roman Adventure

One day, a boy named Rick was walking through a jungle when he fell into a time capsule, which took him to ancient Rome. When they finished building the Colosseum, Rick went to check it. It was *huge!* Around 50,000 people could fit inside. Rick remembered Mum saying, "The Colosseum was finished in 70BC!"
He wandered around the city.
"How much does food cost?" Rick asked himself. He went to a shop and found that food was exchanged for gold or other items. Rick went back home in the time capsule. *What an adventurous day I've had,* Rick thought.

Kavya Kedia (7)
Pontprennau Primary School, Pontprennau

Da Vinci's Problem

It was a sunny day in Italy. It was 18 degrees outside and Leonardo da Vinci was offering portraits to the town. Mona Lisa walked into the shop.

"Hello, my dear lady."

"Hello," she said as she sat down.

"Please smile," Leo said.

She gave him a mean look. He tried everything until a pigeon crashed into the window. Surprised, he snapped his brush and fell headfirst into a bucket of paint and bottom first into a bucket of water! She laughed and laughed, and that's how he got that extra weird, famous smile.

Jack Parker (7)
Pontprennau Primary School, Pontprennau

Blast From The Past

Stars danced before my eyes. A comet hurtled past and a beam of light from a majestic meteoroid hit my face. This was an incredible experience. For the first time, I truly appreciated space's beauty. I was heading towards a place where no human had been before - the moon. Somehow, I had ended up messing around with time (I wanted more time for homework) and I was now stuck fifty years in the past! I didn't regret it; this was a million times better than the 1969 moon landing we had learnt about in school!

Aryav Khurana (8)
Pontprennau Primary School, Pontprennau

Roman Times

The Romans sailed across the sea, taking land after land with their swords. The next stop was a small island called Britain. As they approached the beach, they could see people on the cliffs with their faces painted and holding swords and shields. All that was heard were boatloads of Roman soldiers laughing. The Romans ruled the world so they thought fighting people with their faces painted would be easy, they were wrong. The Celts were fearless fighters and the fighting lasted for many years.

Lilly-Mai Ford (8)
Pontprennau Primary School, Pontprennau

The Ramyana Story

The great king Dasharatha lived in a faraway kingdom with his three wives and four sons. Once, while his eldest son Ram was travelling, he won the hand of a beautiful princess, Sita.

Later, a wicked, mean maid tried to persuade one of the wives to make Bharat the king, not Ram. That wife asked for two wishes - that Ram stay in a forest for fourteen years and that he wouldn't be king. The king fainted. Sita and Ram went for fourteen years, then they came back...

Jahnavi Batra (8)
Pontprennau Primary School, Pontprennau

The Dinosaur Fight

One day, there was a raptor. He wandered around the battlefield. Suddenly, a T-rex jumped out of the crumbly bushes. He roared as loud as a hurricane! Suddenly, a stegosaurus jumped out of the wavy brown and green trees. The T-rex charged at the raptor. The raptor ran and ran and ran! All the dinosaurs chased the raptor. Suddenly, a triceratops found him. The triceratops had big horns. The T-rex had tiny arms. Suddenly, the volcano erupted and they were all extinct.

Beth Parker (8)
Pontprennau Primary School, Pontprennau

The Treasure

One day, I was climbing a snowy mountain and found a cave. I was committed to enter. The cave was cold, dark and damp. The icicles were ready to fall. I started walking and came across what looked like a lair. There was a pile on the floor, like a bed. Scared, I ran out of the cave. I then saw a mummy and daddy mammoth calling for help. I could see a baby mammoth stuck under ice. I had to help. I rescued it by cracking the ice and pulling it out.

Charlie Lewys Cummings (8)
Pontprennau Primary School, Pontprennau

World War Two

"Sir!" shouted the major. "We have had news. News from the front line. All our planes have been shot down, sir."

"Never!" bawled the general. "We needed those planes!"

"I'm not a pilot, sir."

"Well, call the RAF then!"

"Yes, sir. Right away, sir."

Meanwhile, the RAF were flying their Spitfires, Hurricanes and Lancaster bombers.

"Right," said the squadron leader, "all Spitfires advance. Bombers on the right, Hurricanes on the left. Hitler's forces will be along soon."

"Yes, sir. Right away, sir."

"Now let's take them down!" cheered the squadron leader.

Gabriel Gale (8)
Redhill Preparatory School, Haverfordwest

The Story Competition

Have you ever wondered what dinosaurs did in their spare time?

Once, there was a dinosaur story competition. The T-rex told a story about how to run with tiny arms. The stegosaurus told a story about why her plates changed colour, and the triceratops told a story on which plants were healthy for dinosaurs. The judges couldn't decide which story was the best. The T-rex insisted that his was the best, but the others thought theirs were better. They argued for 187 million years, then they began to announce the winner. *Bang!* The competition was over, the dinosaurs disappeared.

Annabel John (9)
Redhill Preparatory School, Haverfordwest

The Pirate's Adventure

It was a blazing hot day. Charles the pirate sailed to land, but he didn't know he was going to Turkey. In Turkey, he found a girl called Molly and some amazing treasure.

Molly said, "Can I come with you? I'll do all of the work!"

"Yes," he said.

Molly went with the pirate.

A few hours later, the pirate felt really ill. Molly was then in charge of cleaning, cooking, making the medicine and controlling the boat.

After a couple of weeks, the pirate was much better. He thanked the girl so much for looking after him.

Megan Bateman (9)
Redhill Preparatory School, Haverfordwest

The Plague Is Coming

I was walking along the dirty streets of London. Suddenly, I heard a bell ring.
"The plague is coming! Quick, go back into your house!"
Nobody knew what he was talking about so we just carried on walking. Suddenly, I saw what was going on, so I ran back inside my house. That man was telling the truth! A herd of rats started swarming everywhere. Everyone ran into their houses, but some were too late. Rats started running up humans' sleeves. Some even got knocked to the ground, knowing that the rat had picked them. They were at death's door...

Katie John (9)
Redhill Preparatory School, Haverfordwest

The Vikings

Lightning tore open the sky as the Viking longboat cut through the crashing waves.
"Come on, men, row!" ordered the Viking chief.
"We need to get to Norway as fast as we can so we can rule the place. Ha!"
Two months later, they arrived in Norway. They stepped on land, ready to fight the boss of Norway with swords and shields. The Viking warriors were anxious. The Viking chief said, "Attack!"
Then the battle started. One warrior snuck through the enemies, then saw something shiny in the palace; it was gold!

Pirasanna Akshayan (8)
Redhill Preparatory School, Haverfordwest

Viking Village

One day at Viking Village, three Vikings went hunting. They normally took five to eight hours, but they never came back. The other Vikings went to search for them but as much as they tried, they couldn't find them. So they made a rumour, they said there was a dragon and it captured the three hunters. Everybody believed it and nobody went hunting that way again... Until sixteen brave hunters in 1079 tried to find the dragon and avenge their fellow hunters.

Hours later, only one came back alive, shouting, "The myth is true!"

Ioan Connor Ireland (10)
Redhill Preparatory School, Haverfordwest

Has Queen Victoria Really Passed Away?

A long time ago, Queen Victoria passed away, but is this true? Some people think she died, some people think she was kidnapped; they are all wrong. This is how it all happened.

One day, Queen Victoria was getting tired of signing laws and being famous, she didn't know what to do about it. She finally thought of something. She thought, *what if she faked her own death?*

When everybody found out, they were devastated. Since then, scientists have dug up her grave. Nobody is in there, leaving us to wonder where she is...

Isabella Crystal Lily Harries (10)
Redhill Preparatory School, Haverfordwest

The Titanic

I was so excited! The Titanic was departing from Southampton the next day. I was one of the first people to board the Titanic on the 10th April, 1912 at midday.

When we departed, I was shown to my cabin; the best part was seeing the grand, sweeping staircase.

I arrived in my cabin and it was calm and peaceful for four days until 11:40pm, when the entire ship shook.

I heard someone shout, "We have hit an iceberg!"

I started to run out of my cabin and run to the emergency lifeboats. I was lucky I survived!

Bethan Lusher (10)
Redhill Preparatory School, Haverfordwest

The Fright And The Relief

It was night in ancient Egypt. I was alone. A shiver ran down my back. The ground started rumbling. I heard twigs snap behind me. A rock landed beside me. I picked it up and examined it. It was cold and bumpy. A shadow loomed over me. The next thing I knew, I was tied up in bandages! I looked up. A mummy was stood in front of me; he had twinkly blue eyes, he said his name was Onterow.
"Please don't tell anyone I'm alive," he said in a grumbly voice.
We made friends. I visited him every night!

Seren Kaill (9)
Redhill Preparatory School, Haverfordwest

The Dinosaurs

The sandy desert blew onto the trees as the boy ran for his life from the dinosaurs. Unfortunately, he tripped over a pinecone and the dinosaurs surrounded the boy. He was trying to escape but one of the dinosaurs was guarding the boy.

After a while, when the sky was pitch-black, all of the dinosaurs were asleep but the boy was in the room locked up.

After a while, the boy was thinking. He looked around the room. On the floor was a sharp stick. He got the stick and tried to get out. Eventually, he got out.

Sangavi Rajaseelan (9)
Redhill Preparatory School, Haverfordwest

The Plague

The pale light of dawn filled my vision as the world shrank. This was the moment my life came to an end.
I had been investigating the cause of death of all these people. The mystery of the Great Plague had almost been unravelled in my mind. It was something to do with the rats. People thought I was crazy, but I was sure I was right. I heard something that sounded like my grandfather screaming.
"I must be dreaming," I said to myself, but 'I love you' were the last words I ever heard.

Kathryn Elin Thomas (9)
Redhill Preparatory School, Haverfordwest

Deep In The Pyramids

As I stepped into the cold, misty tomb, I saw millions of jewels like glinting eyes in the darkness. My knee hit something hard - a coffin. The lid started glowing. It rose up off the coffin. I ran for my life!
I was telling myself, "Don't look back."
I *had* to! I looked back, my blood ran cold. He had now got up out of the coffin and was chasing me. He was gaining speed quickly. My head hit something freezing - a dead end! Was I going to die? The mummy was looming over me...

Isabella Frost (8)
Redhill Preparatory School, Haverfordwest

The Great Fire Of London

On 2nd September, 1666, Thomas Farriner's bakery was closing down for the day. The street that the shop was on was called Pudding Lane. That day, the owner left the oven on in the shop and it set alight. Then the flame got bigger until the flame became a fire! It burnt down the whole shop and then set light to the other buildings nearby because they were made of wood. The fire rage through the city.

After a few days, the fire was under control and luckily, only six people died in the fire.

Lily Lawrence (11)
Redhill Preparatory School, Haverfordwest

Run For It

As I travelled to Westminster, the rain was falling down like a hail of arrows on the roof of the carriage. I said to the king I'd lock up the palace, but I did something else.

He came down the oak hall smashing windows, slamming the doors, banging his feet. He came stamping into the kitchen.

"Where is she?" demanded King Henry, but I was gone.

I ran that night and got away.

Finally, I was home, looking at the scroll I'd stolen, until I heard a knock on the door...

Isabella Vickers (9)
Redhill Preparatory School, Haverfordwest

The Explorer

The sand was hot and dry. The explorer was walking in a desert but he had nothing to guide him. Suddenly, he stepped on a point. The explorer dug it up and saw it was a pyramid. He went into it, then the explorer saw a golden medal and took it. Suddenly, the pyramid went upside down and slowly sank into the sand. The explorer ran for his life, trying to find an exit. The explorer was tired. He opened a door and a mummy came running after him! Then he stepped on something...
"Argh!"

Harry Thomas (8)
Redhill Preparatory School, Haverfordwest

Hunting

It's May. I am Commander Cody Iron Wall, commanding King George V's ship. My mission is to hunt and sink Bismarck. My fear is my ship will go down with my crew. A few are new and a few are old. Jim is one of the oldest of the lads. We should be engaging in a few minutes.

Boom! Bang! This will be a tough battle. We fire again. Our planes are soaring from home base. We pick up a few of our pilots who were shot down. This will be a tough battle, but hopefully, we will win...

Sam Hutton (9)
Redhill Preparatory School, Haverfordwest

The Evil Ancient Egyptian Mummy

I heard something, it was a noise I'd never heard before. I saw something, it was getting closer so I turned away and ran. I felt a scratch on my back and turned around. It had huge sharp teeth with glowing green eyes and it was covered in blood, but I didn't know what it was because it had a black cape over its clothes. I ran for my life, sprinting like mad. Then it pulled and pushed me onto the floor. I screamed but nobody came. It took its cape off and I realised it was a mummy...

Ali Gouda (10)
Redhill Preparatory School, Haverfordwest

War!

Bang! The bomb formed a crater as my mind raced back to where my life changed forever. It was 1939 when the guns started to shoot, rapidly destroying cover and killing people.

"Fire!" shouted the major.

The siren sounded and I could tell that the enemy was moving, so I looked behind me to see bombs landing on the village. I looked back at the battlefield and I saw an endless pile of corpses. Finally, in 1945, Britain and its allies defeated the enemy.

Finlay McQueen (9)
Redhill Preparatory School, Haverfordwest

The Plague Doctor

I am a plague doctor. Trust me, being a plague doctor is hard work because you have to walk around on the dirty streets with blood everywhere and hear bells ringing 24/7 and also wear a really uncomfortable white robe made out of some kind of material. When patients come to me, I don't really know the cure, I just get a big sharp stick and use that to try and pop their big bumps full of watery stuff like pus! Since I was little, I've always pretended to be a plague doctor.

Deema Al-Samra (10)
Redhill Preparatory School, Haverfordwest

Rosa Parks

April, 1946. A lady was walking down the street to her bus. She was wearing a black skirt, a white shirt and a navy cardigan. She got on bus number 340. She sat down but ten minutes later, one more person got on and asked her to get off because she was black. But she refused to so the other person told the bus driver. The bus driver told Rosa Parks to move but she refused and got arrested.
When she got out of prison, she kept on doing the same thing again and again.

Erin Frost (10)
Redhill Preparatory School, Haverfordwest

WWII

I was about to unload out of my warship but there was a land mine right under our boat. *Bang!* The ship blew to pieces whilst we were flooding out. I was finally on the beach and I took a look at the great disaster. I shot at a group of Nazis who were protecting the beach. I took the warriors down and attacked the town. I saw a big group of Nazis crowded around someone. It was Adolf Hitler. I looked behind me and someone had crept behind me. It was a Nazi...

Freddie Watson-Miller (10)
Redhill Preparatory School, Haverfordwest

Ancient Egypt

The blazing hot sun beat down on me as I approached the tomb. I held my breath as I crept down the sandy staircase into the damp chamber. I was terrified. I searched the tomb until I found Tutankhamun's sarcophagus. I was so happy but suddenly, I felt a figure brush past my shoulder. I realised I wasn't alone! I ran for my life. I could feel the figure getting closer. Then suddenly, I saw that I was trapped! I turned around and held my breath...

Harri Coaker (9)
Redhill Preparatory School, Haverfordwest

Captured

July 1941. Name: Sgt Iron. I'd just got in the trench, Chief told me I needed to go and sneak onto the hill behind the Nazi's main base. I took a small tent in my backpack and I could sort of hear what they were saying. I went back to the trench, then I fell asleep.

When I woke up, I ran back to my tent on the hill behind the Nazi base. One of the Nazis saw me. Luckily, I could talk German really well, but they didn't believe me...

Max Ironside (10)
Redhill Preparatory School, Haverfordwest

The Fainting Queen

One day, Queen Victoria fainted in shock! Her personal servant was packing her things to leave. What would she do? She'd have to find one. Who wanted the job of the queen's servant? Nobody wanted to be her servant. She was sad. At midnight, someone knocked at the door. No one answered it so she went to answer the door. There was a beautiful young lady saying, "I am here for the job."

"Weehaw!" shouted the queen.

Emma Edwards (8)
Redhill Preparatory School, Haverfordwest

The Ancient Tomb

As I put my head down on the cold stone slab, my mind raced back twenty years, to the night my life changed forever.

I recalled lightning in the sky as I crept down into the shadows. I heaved the body out of the sarcophagus and slowly shuffled out until I heard them. Voices. I made a run for it. I heard a flash as the air was cut behind me. I ran into hiding. I was caught on this cool, misty night; the night they got their tomb god back.

Charles Muehlbauer (9)
Redhill Preparatory School, Haverfordwest

The Mummy And The Little Girl

A little girl saw a tomb and got scared. She opened the tomb. A mummy jumped out and scared the little girl. She ran away. She didn't know what to do so she grabbed a rope and swung the rope and caught the mummy. But the mummy was so strong, she got out of the rope. The mummy ran so fast, the little girl ran away from her. Then the little girl trapped the mummy and it was never to be seen ever again!

Darcy Louise Flynn (8)
Redhill Preparatory School, Haverfordwest

Egypt

The adventurer was finding clues. One day, he found a pyramid and went inside. But something came out of the sarcophagus. Inside the sarcophagus was a mummy! Everybody ran away from it. Eventually, everyone got out, except for the adventurer. The adventurer was caught and the mummy put the adventurer into the sarcophagus. Then the adventurer snuck out of the sarcophagus and ran out of the pyramid.

Seth Appleby (8)
Redhill Preparatory School, Haverfordwest

Mummies

The bad mummies went to kill all the good mummies. One of them saw a staff when the good mummies got back from the forest. The bad mummies went to kill them and they had a big battle. The staff helped the good mummies to kill the bad mummies. So the good mummies went back to their home and to rebuild their village. Then the good mummies went to kill the bad mummies' boss.

Charlie Hughes (10)
Redhill Preparatory School, Haverfordwest

Fight For Everyone's Lives

In the trenches of Wales, I was fighting for my life. There were gunshots everywhere and bloody bodies all over the place. I started to see a bomb coming straight towards me. A soldier came running to yank me to the side and started shooting the opposition. Then I saw loads of soldiers jumping over the trench. They started running closer and closer to the enemies' trench. As they scrambled to get in the trench, they started shooting every soldier in their paths. They threw grenades everywhere and found their bunker and wrecked everything. They won the Great War!

Ruairi Harris (10)
St David's RC Primary School, West Cross

The Great Fire Of London

My life was at risk. I couldn't cope with the ruby fire burning the village houses to ash. No time to run from the blazing fire destroying everything in its path. My heart was pondering and racing like the cold howling wind during a full moon. My family rushed and pushed to get to the filthy, disgusting basement. It was dark and freezing cold. Suddenly, I heard a crash and a smash. It sounded like thunder. Nothing could stop the roaring, scorching fire as it took everyone's prized possessions as well as people. Rocks crumbled down - destruction!

Lucy Maslen (10)
St David's RC Primary School, West Cross

Terrible Tudors

The executions began to take place. One by one, they proceeded to the chopping block. Their heads were decapitated like ants being crushed by cruel children. Henry VIII was still enjoying the moment after everyone had left.

The following day, he ordered the execution of his head servant and Anne Boleyn, who too went to the chopping block, decapitated by a swordsman from Spain. Anne, who he had loved so much, had disappointed him giving him a daughter rather than the son he longed for. Each day, Henry ordered more deaths and more blood was spilt...

Rhun Hywel Mugford (10)
St David's RC Primary School, West Cross

Big Blue Monster

As I sprinted through the bushy trees, running faster than ever, the big monster chased after me. My blood pressure was escalating and my footsteps grew immensely. Suddenly, I stopped. I couldn't go any further. There was a cliff. The giant beast stomped, knocking down trees as it came in front of me. I saw my life flashing in front of me: my mum, my dad, my brother. The beast was a dinosaur. It approached, ready to eat me. I jumped. As I glided through the air, I was relieved but I realised I was nearing the ground, closer... closer...

Mia Denti Richards (10)
St David's RC Primary School, West Cross

The Mummies

The Egyptian tomb was shuddering loudly as the pharaoh opened his tomb. The tomb was creaking thunderously as I saw the pharaoh's head. I ran as fast as I could, looking for somewhere to hide. There was a large tomb filled with intimidating spiderwebs. I opened it and saw another mummy moving. I sprinted for my life. My heart was pounding. The pharaoh's mummies were chasing me, using their stiff-like walk. As I ran, I saw a door. It was covered in Egyptian writing. In the blink of an eye, I was face-to-face with more mummies...

Eloghosa Ikpomwosa-Aghedo (10)
St David's RC Primary School, West Cross

The Black Death

The time had come. Everybody I knew had gone. I had to run away. Everywhere I walked, there were dead, lifeless people covered in boils strewn all over the rotten floor. I packed my bags and headed towards the Thames. I heard there were boats going to Spain. The Black Death wasn't so bad there. As I walked to the boats, I noticed the flea-bitten rats crawling like spiders all over the streets. I was appalled! I boarded the boat to Spain. It wasn't much cleaner than the streets. I exited the boat but I knew I wasn't safe...

Isabella Cushion (10)
St David's RC Primary School, West Cross

Dino Cove

I stepped into Dino Cove. It was covered in moss and leaves. I walked on, stepping over the cracks cautiously and quickly. Suddenly, the path vanished and I walked to the edge. My stomach tightened. My heart was pumping. *Roar!* I froze. I was sure I heard a roar. I turned around. My stomach clenched. I was almost face-to-face with a dinosaur, approaching behind me. My heart skipped a beat. Then I ran, but soon enough, I realised I was running in the air. I screamed as I fell. There was silence. I disappeared into the darkness.

Sofia Elena Ramos (10)
St David's RC Primary School, West Cross

Pharaoh's Fury

Outside the scruffy pyramid, that's where I stood. My trembling feet took a scared step, my brain told my scared feet to run like the wind. My sense of adventure was dying by the second. My head was spinning... By the time I had stopped running, I was in a filthy pharaoh's tomb and there stood a big, old, gold coffin. I slid my tender, shivering fingers through. I pulled and pulled. The lid collapsed and there it was. It stepped out. My heart dropped. My jaw unhinged. I ran like the wind, but it followed me like a shadow...

Daniel Hughes (10)
St David's RC Primary School, West Cross

Pointy Pyramid

In the middle of a sandy desert was a pyramid. It was hotter than the sun. I entered the pyramid. There were traps everywhere. I passed all of the traps. I made it! In front of me was the tomb. I could smell rats. I could see dust and cobwebs, but then I realised the tomb was open. I gulped and clenched my hands. I looked for an exit but couldn't find one. I was trapped with no escape. There, in front of me, was the mummy. Suddenly, it raced forward, menacingly attacking me with its horrible, stiff hands.

Joshua Ellis Evans (10)
St David's RC Primary School, West Cross

The Roman Troop

As Gary walked along the forest, he suddenly got attacked. He had his troop battle them. He ran as soon as possible, rustling every leaf in his path. They caught up; the horrible, disgusting beasts. He managed to kill all but one, the most fierce and cruel; the leader, Celt. He threw Gary back and forth. As Gary slid his only chance out, he plunged his sword into the Celt's chest. He thought he had won but no, he hadn't. He found his troop in pools of blood. He was sad but finally, he had won.

Ellis James Williams (10)
St David's RC Primary School, West Cross

Cells

I was there with my best friend, Louis. We were preparing to take on the Romans. We went screaming into battle, suddenly I lost Louis in the heap of it. I was running, trying to find my best friend. The commander was searching, then he stopped. I looked up, He was dead, I felt sick but I carried on. I came face-to-face with a Roman who wanted to kill me. Suddenly, he fell to his knees. The archers had shot him. I kept looking. Next, a rock hit me on the head, I looked and saw my friend was dead...

Luca Jenson Armani (10)
St David's RC Primary School, West Cross

The Beast Is Here

The wind howled as the monster approached. My heart stopped, trees rustled and as I looked up, I saw the horrible anger in his eyes and blood on its teeth. I sprinted for my life! The beast chased me. *Roar!* I clutched my hands and hid behind a tree, catching my breath. I screamed, then the monster came closer and closer. All of a sudden, I was in the air and I just made it out alive. It was terrifying. My heart was pounding. I did not know what to do, then I was saved by a pterodactyl.

Tom Joseph Hedden (10)
St David's RC Primary School, West Cross

The Dark Creepy Forest

My father said it was time to go and hunt for a boar. He gave me a spear and his sword. It is hard being a Celt, not only do I have to hunt, but also avoid my enemy the Romans.

I walked into the forest. The wind howled, the trees rustled. My heart pounded. Suddenly, behind was a Roman. I drew my sword - was I going to survive? Later, at my feet lay the dead Roman. I came to hunt and kill a boar, but instead had killed my first Roman. I couldn't wait to tell my father.

Eve Evans (10)
St David's RC Primary School, West Cross

World War Two

My hands were shaking and sweaty. We were almost at the beach. I was nervous but ready. When we got to the beach, there was a shower of gunfire. Some of us didn't make it, but others got away.

A few minutes later, we were shooting down our enemies.

Later, I found a town. Everybody was in hiding except for one, who came up to us to tell us that a tank was coming. The tank shot the guy in the tower, killing him. The tank shot, a high building fell, crushing everyone.

Patrick Rawls (10)
St David's RC Primary School, West Cross

Ancient Egypt

My heart was pounding as I entered the unlit tomb. I could barely see. I soon felt a warm breath behind me. As I turned around, my head felt like it was going to explode. It was blazing hot. I felt like I was going to faint. I suddenly saw a glowing circle. I sprinted as fast as I could towards it. As I picked it up, I saw gold, blue and strange markings drenched in diamonds and pearls. I managed to pry it open. Suddenly, the air was filled with a menacing, horrible gas...

Eva Rowlands (10)
St David's RC Primary School, West Cross

The Tomb Raider

In a dark tomb, the tomb raider was searching for a bar of gold. He had succeeded in getting the gold, but then the only door started to close. He was in fear, but then he had an idea. So he jammed the door with the gold, but the gold got crushed! He tried to open the door but it was too dark to see anything, then he forgot where the door was. He was scared, sad and a little mad. He tried to get out but he was locked in. Then another raider opened the door and helped him.

Oisin Tobin (10)
St David's RC Primary School, West Cross

The Mummy In The Tomb

I was in a tomb. It was dark. The museum archaeologist was with me. Suddenly, the tomb reverberated. We had awoken the mummy with red eyes and a bandaged body. It chased after us. We got out and jumped into the car and left the tomb. The mummy chased us. The mummy was running. We went all over Egypt with a mummy on our tail. We went back to the tomb. We climbed back in. I found some dynamite. I lit the match and put the match on the string. We ran out quickly.

Hannah Kielthy (10)
St David's RC Primary School, West Cross

Angry Aztecs

In the tropical summer, the sun never set. I woke up to see an Aztec man outside screaming some kind of ritual, which was freaky but what I saw during the ritual was even eerier. There was a heart in the middle of the circle. The heart was beating. I was starting to question if it was all a bad dream. But then it hit me. They were doing rituals to sacrifice me to their king to worship him. *Thump... thump...* My heart was pounding. Was I going to die?

Samit Sajeev (10)
St David's RC Primary School, West Cross

My Prey

I saw my prey with its beady black eyes and patterned skin. As I clambered into a bush where I could watch my prey, it went to rest. I pounced out of the bush. It got up and ran like the wind. I sprinted after it. As it lost its pace, I went in to kill the sabre-toothed tiger, but then something bigger approached behind me... a monster! I dropped my spear and ran for my life! It was behind me. I looked it in the eye, then in one gulp, I was gone in a flash.

Matilda Elizabeth Lewis (10)
St David's RC Primary School, West Cross

Ancient Egypt

The gold searcher started looking for gold. He found an old, rusted, mysterious cave. He took a breath and walked fearfully into the cave. *Bam!* He saw glowing eyes in the dark. Next, he saw a mummy! They looked in each other's eyes. With a gulp, he ran out of the cave. He was like a cheetah with two legs. He was running in the hot, burning desert. The sand kept getting in his eyes. He ran into the sunset, not looking back.

Charlie Edwards
St David's RC Primary School, West Cross

Gold Rush

Gold is everyone's dream. Whether it is to make a fortune or just to show off. I heard that Tenochtitlan is the place to find gold, so I'm gonna dig for my own! The Aztec Empire has fallen, but there is still gold in those mines!

As I wearily trudge through the fog-clouded ruins, I stumble across a cemetery; bones crunch underfoot and staring stones lean inwards. At the end of the path, there is a shaft and as I step in, I don't only see gold, I see a lost civilisation of Aztecs, an untouched city!

Madison Bermingham (11)
Treffos Independent School, Llansadwrn

The Midnight Girl

It was a bitter night. All the chimney children were asleep except one boy called Edward. The old grandfather clock chimed midnight and Edward stared into the darkness. Mist swirled in the corner of the room and the ghostly shape of a young girl in a ragged dress appeared.
"Who are you?" Edward whispered.
"I'm Abigail Raymond Thomas, your lost sister."
"My sister?" exclaimed Edward. "What happened to you, are you a ghost?"
Abigail's image blurred and swirled.
"I was sent to the workhouse, where I caught typhoid and died."
Edward felt empty and sad as Abigail left him again.

Freya Hughes (9)
Trelales Primary School, Laleston

Dinosaurs

Once, there were three dinosaurs. Their names were Dena, Dino and Tiny. Dena had enormous, sharp spikes. Dino was fast. Tiny was miniature. One day, they met by the water hole to go hunting. Suddenly, the ground started to shake and bright orange lava erupted from a volcano.

"Run!" screamed Dino.

All of a sudden, huge claws picked them up and whisked them back to a cave.

"Thank you for rescuing us," breathed Tiny.

"That's quite alright," replied the T-rex, "but don't get into any more trouble. Run along now."

The dinosaurs walked back to the comfort of their cave.

Chloe Thomas-Lane (9)
Trelales Primary School, Laleston

The Haunt Of Ogmore Castle

'Twas a freezing morning at Ogmore Castle. You could feel the howling wind through the stone walls. Jack was going off to war.

"Oh Jack, why do you have to go?" cried Lillian.

"I'm doing it for the country," answered Jack in a manly voice.

"Bye," sobbed Lillian sadly.

Jack galloped off on his noble steed.

A few months later, Lillian gave birth to a little girl called Elizabeth. She was a bright child. The months became years and eventually, Lillian and Elizabeth died. They haunt Ogmore Castle still to this day, looking for Jack around the old, broken halls.

Hermione Farmer (9)
Trelales Primary School, Laleston

The Mummy's Curse

It was a cold and scary night. Sean and Gethin were exploring the cobwebbed pyramid when they met Victor, an archaeologist. He showed them to a mummy's tomb.

"This mummy is cursed," said Victor.

"How foolish," whispered Sean, "we all know mummies are dead and can't harm us!"

With that, the mummy rose from the tomb. Sean and Gethin ran as fast as they could. The mummy's bandages unravelled as he chased them. The boys were shaking in fear as they heard the grinding of stone and the doorway of the pyramid close, trapping them in total darkness...

Sean Finnie (8)
Trelales Primary School, Laleston

The Deepest Biggest Jungle

One day, in the deepest, biggest, jungliest jungle ever was the most lime-green coloured dinosaur in history. There was a boy called Benjamin. Benjamin really wanted to find the dinosaur.

The next day, Benjamin went for a hike to find it. Benjamin saw enormous footprints, larger than himself! He followed the enormous footprints until they faded away and stopped. Benjamin felt scared and excited at the same time.

He found the dinosaur and was amazed. But for some reason, it was mad, *furious* even. The dinosaur started chasing him.

"Help!" he cried...

Benjamin Jones (9)
Trelales Primary School, Laleston

The Runaway

Charles sadly walked into his master's house. The door screeched.

"Get up the chimney then, little boy!" shouted Jonathon, his master.

Charles was hungry, tired and frightened. Charles was frightened of the dark and sick of cleaning dusty chimneys. Out of the corner of his eye, he saw a goose on the kitchen table. He hadn't eaten in ages so he got so excited and grabbed the goose and ran. He shot past his master and out of the door. His master chased him but he slipped. There was a loud crack as his leg snapped. Charles was very lucky.

Niamh Hemburrow (9)
Trelales Primary School, Laleston

The Dinosaur Trip

One creepy day, three men were driving through the jungle in their minivan when something caught their eye. It was a rusty, old time machine. The men were amazed and decided to see if it would work. They rubbed the colourful buttons and brushed off the rust. Just as they sat on the round metal seat to have a rest, a dinosaur appeared. It had sharp teeth, an enormous mouth and two red horns sticking out of its spiky head. They panicked, pressed the blue 'stop' button and the time machine vanished, but the dinosaur was still standing there...

Mason Brown (9)
Trelales Primary School, Laleston

Boudicca And The Romans

Boudicca was ready for the battle against the Romans with her army. The battle went on for days and weeks. It was very scary and super tiring but they did not stop. Thousands were killed. It was very sad. People left their families and friends.
It started to rain so one of the Romans shouted, "Battle will carry on in the morning!"
The battle carried on for days again. The Romans won and they beat Boudicca and her daughters so Boudicca poisoned herself because she was humiliated. The Celts missed her, it was very sad.

Rosie Harry (9)
Trelales Primary School, Laleston

Safe

I climbed up the soggy chimney. My legs were aching! I could hear my master shouting through all the soot. Finally, I could see the light of day peeking through the top of the chimney. I could feel small butterflies in my tummy. Suddenly, I felt warmth on my legs and thighs. I peeked down, there was a blazing fire below me! Smoke billowed. I climbed as fast as I could. Coughing, I made it to the top of the chimney.
As I climbed out, I heard my master shouting, "Get down!"
I didn't want to. I felt safe...

Delyth Foster (9)
Trelales Primary School, Laleston

D-Day

All we knew was we were going to land on a beach. The alarm was screeching. We were invading a beach in France. Machine guns fired. It was like hell! One by one, my friends were sniped. Forever, it would stay with me. Opening the hatch, there were dead bodies everywhere. I was terrified. Blood stained the water. I shot everything that moved in the German trenches. I charged in the trench with my bayonet. The Germans surrendered but some shot themselves so they couldn't tell us anything. Many soldiers died.

Ioan Hughes Davies (9)
Trelales Primary School, Laleston

The Scared Celt

In the distance, the Romans were screaming fiercely. The little Celt was scared to death.
His mother said, "Be brave."
So he stood up and said, "I must be brave."
The Romans were throwing spears of fire! One landed on the roundhouse. Bits of the roundhouse were collapsing.
"Run!" screamed the mother.
The Romans were waiting outside, ready to fight. The little Celt fought bravely.
Eventually, all the Romans were dead. The fort was safe again, hooray!

Thomas Edward Morgan (9)
Trelales Primary School, Laleston

Invasion Of The Beach

Jim and James were on the beach with their pet, Riddle Star, when the Romans invaded. Jim hid behind a huge rockpool, then a Roman crept up and hit him with a spear. Jim turned, grabbed the weapon and wounded him. The Roman was bleeding and in pain. The tide came and washed the crimson blood away. The Celts marched onto the sand and helped Jim to safety. They collected figwort from the forest and used it to heal his wounds. The other Celtic warriors fought a battle on the beach against the Romans and won.

Jake Hamilton (9)
Trelales Primary School, Laleston

The Mummy Hunt

One dreary morning in the pyramid, the world-famous archaeologist Howard Carter was searching for mummies. Suddenly, his trowel whacked something hard and shiny. He blew all the dust off.

"I'll be rich," he whispered.

Howard Carter opened the sarcophagus and on the side of it, there were hieroglyphics. A mummy appeared next to him with a sword in its wrapped hand. Howard Carter fell to the floor in pain. His eyes reflected the mummy's still, cold heart and then darkness...

Gracie Kearns (9)
Trelales Primary School, Laleston

The Pterodactyl Dome

Finally, the new dinosaur park was open. I felt excited and was hopping with joy! I was going there for a birthday treat and couldn't wait! Scientists had recreated living dinosaurs in their natural habitat by using DNA from fossils.

When we entered, we saw a monorail and jumped on quickly. It whisked us to an island and we got off and walked towards the pterodactyl's dome. It was enormous and we could hear the dinosaurs screeching in a frightened way. Something was wrong...

Gethin Lewis Narbeth (9)
Trelales Primary School, Laleston

Dino Attack

One roasting day in the jungle in the dinosaur times, I stood alone. I felt exhausted on the outside and ill from the heat on the inside. So I jumped into the river to cool down a bit. In the river, I saw a crab, fish, seaweed and an octopus.

Soon after, I hung my clothes on a peg and got changed. I was sitting down at the time when something huge nudged me. It was a dinosaur, an enormous beast with sharp teeth that growled at me. I could feel its breath on my neck...

Callum Joseph Threfall (9)
Trelales Primary School, Laleston

Poor Boy

One cold, misty day, my master told me to climb another dark, dusty chimney. My heart began to pound. My body shook and tears pricked my sooty eyes. I was frightened but had no choice. I wriggled up into the filthy space and climbed until I reached the roof. It was high and the wind had begun to blow. Below, I could see everything. I could see the sun rising and loads of buildings and the sky. It was lovely. I said in my head, *I wish I could stay here forever.*

Coby Jervis (9)
Trelales Primary School, Laleston

The Mummy Case

On a hot day, a boy called Cole went into a scary pyramid. Cole stepped in and there was a mummy case dripping with lava. Suddenly, the case started to creak. Cole was terrified, then a mummy came out.
It shouted, "Run!"
Cole was so scared his legs were shaking!
Then the mummy whispered, "You are in danger, run!"
Cole ran around the pyramid, through the exit and decided never to go exploring again.

Jake Ellams (9)
Trelales Primary School, Laleston

The Robbery

Once, there was a very rich man who got his money from his chimney sweeps.
One night, he heard a noise. He thought it was the wind. Then he heard it again, so he went to investigate downstairs. He saw a child with money. "Come here you lil' rat!" He chased him to a derelict park. The boy was fast and got away. And for once, the boys and his friends could afford to buy food.

William Waite (9)
Trelales Primary School, Laleston

The Bullet

Bang! A bullet flew towards MLK. I'm Skylar and I was sadly there when Martin Luther King got shot. He was a knight in shining armour fighting the dragon of inequality.

"Argh, he has no pulse!" said the nurse.

We were at the hospital.

"He was shot in the nose with a Remington rifle," said Neon, my BFF.

"It was James Earl Ray, let's get him and avenge MLK!" said a doctor.

A crowd gathered at the police station.

"Get him!" screamed the crowd, pointing at James Earl Ray.

The chase began...

Izzy Ellie Bartram (10)
Ysgol Bro Ingli, Newport

The Living Mummy

It was a cold night and in a sand temple lay a crusty ancient tomb. It had mould and looked atrocious.

One evening, a tourist roamed around. He saw the coffin and opened it. A mummy miraculously sprang out. The man was gone in a second. The mummy proceeded to follow the man but eventually lost him. She looked up to see where she was. There was a huge, tall building and futuristic hover cars. She wondered where she was. Then she noticed it was the future! She quickly panicked and ran back to her tomb.

Alex English (10)
Ysgol Bro Ingli, Newport

Bob And The Mummy

The wind outside the cave howled and every breath Bob took echoed around the cave. Bob heard a crunch and realised he had stood on the bone of a human! A shiver went down his spine.
"Who is there?" said a voice from further in the cave.
Suddenly, a bat came out of nowhere and hit him on the head.
He woke up. He was lying down on the floor next to a drop so deep he could not see the bottom! A mummy was standing in front of him. Bob got up and shoved the mummy off the edge.

Hari Nambisan (11)
Ysgol Bro Ingli, Newport

The Bad Stones

My feet started to hurt walking along this burning, painful path, so I got an idea - *what if we make something flat to walk on?* I told the other villagers and asked for their opinion. They thought it was a good idea because their feet hurt as well, so I talked to some builders to make it happen. They asked what the name of my idea was.
I said, "It's called a road."
Three weeks later and this road still hurt my feet, it now burnt like the sun!

Nathaniel Elmes (11)
Ysgol Bro Ingli, Newport

The Pyramid Adventure

It was a hot day. The golden sand was like fire beneath my feet. The sun shone high over the ancient pyramids. The priceless treasure lay somewhere inside. I walked for hours through dark tunnels filled with dreadful drawings.

Finally, I reached a gigantic, circular room lined with hundreds of gold sarcophagi covered in creepy cobwebs. In the middle of the room shimmered a ruby the size of my fist. I went to grab the gem. As soon as I touched it, the sound of doors opening filled the room. I scooped up the ruby and ran for my life.

Peni Macy (9)
Ysgol Gynradd Mynach, Devils Bridge

The Two Roman Soldiers

One day, Steve and John were on night work. Their job was to guard the big Roman fortress from enemies. They were Roman soldiers and they were the best soldiers around - strong and quick.

It was a cold, windy night and it was freezing. They were keeping watch. Suddenly, they saw a distance light and it was coming closer. In fear of an attack, they raised the alarm. Everyone woke up and everybody got their swords, ready for battle. As the light got closer, they saw that it was just a soldier that had got lost!

Tomos Hopkins (8)
Ysgol Gynradd Mynach, Devils Bridge

Until I Bumped Into Something...

Walking on the stony path in the middle of the dark, scary night, I heard strange noises coming from somewhere. Carrying on walking on the path, a mummy jumped out of nowhere.
"Argh!" I screamed in shock.
I ran as fast as I could in fear that the mummy would catch me, but where was I going? I couldn't see a single thing because the sky was dark. Still running as fast as I could, I bumped into something hard. I looked up and couldn't believe what I saw. There was a knight...

Elain Jenkins (11)
Ysgol Gynradd Mynach, Devils Bridge

The Good Old Days

In Ystwyth Valley, the river ran through mountains. Spine and Rex were on opposite sides of the river. Then forty pterodactyls swept down the river to Spine. They stared at each other. The mountains were so quiet. Rex and Spine looked at the mountains and roared.

Later, they fought the forty pterodactyls. They scared off the pterodactyls but later, they came back. They happily scared them away for good, then they played in the river and had a lot of fun splashing around.

Alfie Fredrick Herbert (9)
Ysgol Gynradd Mynach, Devils Bridge

The Mummy Curse

A long time ago in a pyramid in Egypt, there was a tomb. Two people went to see it called Steve and Pearl. The two opened the tomb. There was a mummy! She wanted to put a curse on them. They came up with an idea; one would distract her, the other would come up behind her and pull the wrap off the mummy. After that, they did it. The two succeeded.
Meanwhile, they went back and kept it a secret.

Laila Hale (9)
Ysgol Gynradd Mynach, Devils Bridge

The Curse Of The Tombs

One night, a pharaoh was drawing in the pyramid when somebody killed him. He was mummified that night. One night was coming up especially for all the mummies to get revenge on whoever killed them. That night was the night. Every mummy's tomb was opening. Whoever killed them would die a few hours later.

The mummies went back into their tombs because it was morning. They never woke again...

Evie Hale (9)
Ysgol Gynradd Mynach, Devils Bridge

Romans Are Coming

There was a girl called Suzane. She lived with her brother, mum and dad in a small roundhouse. One day, Suzane and her brother William went playing in the woods. It was great. All of a sudden, they heard the sound of, "Argh!" It was the Romans!

"Quick, get up a tree!" Suzane shouted.

In the distance, all that could be seen was the Romans. As Suzane looked behind, Celts were stampeding downhill. *Smash!* They crashed into each other.

"Go on, Daddy!" shouted William.

Then their dad pulled out his sword and plunged it through the Romans. Victory was ours.

Harriet Tozer (8)
Ysgol Parcyrhun, Ammanford

The Vikings In The Forest

A girl called Holly was walking in the forest, then she heard the stomping of a thousand feet charging right at her! She turned around and saw about a hundred or so Vikings charging at her! She started running for her life. Her lungs screamed for a break after a while of sprinting. Suddenly, Holly stopped dead in her tracks. One Viking stopped, then they all stopped... Holly looked up to see what looked like a whole army of Anglo-Saxons! They all started charging at each other. She looked the other way and ran back to her safe home.

Rhiane Turton (11)
Ysgol Parcyrhun, Ammanford

Egypt

I went on a school trip to the history museum. I got lost there and couldn't find the rest of my class. I found a time machine with a button that said: *Do Not Touch*, but I still pressed it. There were lots of lights, sounds and smoke. I ended up in Egypt, surrounded by sand, camels and pyramids! There was a maze in one of the pyramids which I had to get through. Once I did, I had to return a golden pharaoh to the king of Egypt, which in return gave me the time machine to return home.

Steffan Rhys Thomas (8)
Ysgol Parcyrhun, Ammanford

The Mean, Deadly Victorians

Leaves crumbled, people screamed in horror as the security of Queen Victoria's palace hunted down a thief that tried to steal the crown. The crown never got stolen but the guards were chasing the thief down because the queen demanded the guards catch the thief and cut off his head as soon as possible.

The guards finally caught the thief and aggressively chopped his head off and threw his body in the bin. After all the exhausting, hard, tiring work, the queen congratulated them and after that, nobody ever dared to break into the queen's palace again.

Kuba Andrzej Mrugala (10)
Ysgol Ty Ffynnon, Shotton

When The Mummies Approached

Winds were low, rivers flowed calmly as could be. With one blink of an eye, the wonders of Egyptians had been seen. With one foot touching the floor, all I could hear was *bang, bang* as one unlucky Egyptian was captured inside the pyramids, banging on the stones, hoping to be set free. I suddenly went into this strange place. I looked around with my heart coming out of my chest. I started running but there was no escape from there. But in the night, all was peaceful. The mummies got into their coffins and the Egyptians went to sleep.

Emmelia Rose Paterson (10)
Ysgol Ty Ffynnon, Shotton

The Dragon Attack

The bloodthirsty dragon roared, burning the village with its molten fire. The silver terror shot its spikes at Arthur, cutting him. He pulled the spikes out and started to bleed. Then a giant red dragon called a flame striker ripped Arthur's red cape, just missing him. The Vikings had all left on their wooden boats without Arthur. He sprinted for the last boat but it had just left. He leapt and hung onto the rim of the boat. The silver terror shot its spikes at Arthur's hands, making him lose grip and fall into the water.

Archie Duncan (10)
Ysgol Ty Ffynnon, Shotton

The Great Battle

A warrior and a knight were called to the throne room in a castle and were told to fight in the war against the army of the mummies, and to defeat the mummy king. So they said they would and they marched through the forest. They saw the enemy team and charged. They defeated the army outside, then fought the mummy king. It was a massive battle but victorious. The knight and the warrior went back to the castle. The king was very happy. He said that the warrior would now be king, so everyone had a big congratulatory party.

Jack Kearns (10)
Ysgol Ty Ffynnon, Shotton

The Day

There was a nice, young, beautiful girl that was a princess. Her name was Alysha. She was kind and pretty.

One day, she planned a wedding. She was really excited. She got married to Ty. They got married in the pyramids. It was the happiest day for her. But then Ty had to go to war!

"Oh no!" said Alysha.

She was really worried about Ty. She was going to try and stop him from going. She had an idea; she would pretend to be sick.

Her plan worked! Ty did not go.

"Yay!"

Tatiana Gorecka (10)
Ysgol Ty Ffynnon, Shotton

World War One

The war had started. The wind was blowing and my feet were damp. I was freezing. I missed my daughter. I wanted to go back to my warm, cosy bed. I heard the bombs drop. *Thud!* All I could hear was ringing. When would this be over? Then a man came running, a bomb hit him. I panicked, I could be next! I sat on the floor and waited, hoping someone would find me. Then everything went silent. My heart dropped to my chest, I was defeated. Then I heard a silent ringing, it got louder... *Thud!*

Isabelle Alâna Jones (10)
Ysgol Ty Ffynnon, Shotton

Spartans Vs Athenians

"For Sparta!" screamed the Spartan leader and his 300 bloodthirsty men, ready to take down the attack of the Athenians. Just a second after, everyone was fighting. Blood was everywhere, dead people were on the ground and weapons were flying. In the end, a little kid called Alexios, part of the Spartans, saw the Athenians kidnapping two people. He picked up a sharp stick and started to assassinate them one by one by hiding in a bush and whistling to lead them into the bush and kill them!

Mariusz Boldowski (10)
Ysgol Ty Ffynnon, Shotton

The Mummy

There were children playing football when they heard a big, massive bang in the dark and gloomy cave next to the green football pitch. They went into the dark and gloomy cave and went deeper and deeper in. Then they saw a dark coffin on the floor. They put it back on the wall, then turned around to go back, but Lily felt a hand on her shoulder.
She turned around slowly and shouted, "It's a mummy!"
They all ran as fast as they could, but the mummy took Tia and disappeared.

Teigan O'Driscoll (10)
Ysgol Ty Ffynnon, Shotton

Viking Mess

With weapons as sharp as knives and Vikings as fierce as dragons, we looked across the village, battling on and on against the Prince of Tigers.
It started when we all worked for Prince of Tigers. He used to boss us around and we'd had enough of being bossed around so we built our own team. Once we did, he didn't like it so Prince of Tigers built another team and battled us.
We just wanted it to stop, so we stopped it. We needed to be friends, so we made friends.

Daniel McHarg (10)
Ysgol Ty Ffynnon, Shotton

Anne Frank's Story

One dark, clear night in the town of Amsterdam, there were deadly guns being fired and H bombs being dropped. They started searching my house so we hid behind the bookshelf.

Years passed with no attacks but that one night, August 4th, 1944, I, Anne Frank, was hiding behind the bookshelf. As we started speaking, a nuke bomb went off and the bookshelf blew up. The Nazis came in and found us going behind the piano. We were sent to Auschwitz, where we later died from typhus.

Hayden Davies (10)
Ysgol Ty Ffynnon, Shotton

World War One

The wind was making sounds through the dark forest. The battle lasted forever. At last, there was silence. Everything was quiet. I thought my friends were alive but they had died and the other half of them were missing. I looked out from my hiding spot. There were people right by me, dead. At that moment, I realised I was the only survivor from this battle.
I went home to my mother all alone. Then I was given the responsibility of working with the beautiful USA.

Victoria Cecot (10)
Ysgol Ty Ffynnon, Shotton

The Mummy War

In the forest one wild, dark night, a crazy Viking was with his pet sasquatch. He set off to start a war with the dreaded mummies.

He found their base and started a war. There were booms and bangs, brains and guts and a lot of blood (he also cut his eye). The war was crazy. *Bang!* The ground exploded. There was a big crack in the Earth for 500 miles!

He found the king mummy and used the mighty god cleaver to win the war. All the mummies were gone!

Aidyn Edward Potter (10)
Ysgol Ty Ffynnon, Shotton

The End

Long, long ago near a really, old, dusty castle lived three Roman soldiers. Their enemies were the Celts. All they ever did was meet up and have fights about who owned the castle.

One day, they went in front of the castle and they fought until one won. Barry was the strongest; he killed the weakest Celt. The second weakest Celt killed a Roman, but then they realised this was pointless so they apologised to each other and they all lived in the castle.

Natalia Sokolowska (10)
Ysgol Ty Ffynnon, Shotton

World War One

It was cold and dark in the war. All I could hear were the bombs dropping down on Britain. All I could do was watch my friends and fellow soldiers die in the war. All I could do was take my final breaths before death. All I could feel was the tears on my face, or was it rain? I didn't know anymore but I felt like the endless tunnel of life was ending for me. As I lay there dying, I had no hope for me. I closed my eyes, hoping for death.

Ella Jane (10)
Ysgol Ty Ffynnon, Shotton